The Ripple Effect

Robert Simpson

An Exciting Look at the Twenty-Third Psalm

THE RIPPLE EFFECT

Second Edition

This edition published in Great Britain in 2024 by
ChristLight Books (a division of the
Sunpenny Publishing Group)

PRINT ISBN: 978-1-907984-44-0

EBOOK ISBN: 978-1-907984-45-7

DEDICATION

To my dear wife Margaret,
whose patient work alongside me
has been my lifeline.

In Praise

I enjoyed reading this book and was touched by what the author wrote... A refreshing journey through the best known and best loved of the psalms.

— *The Reverend Laurence Ennor from the Alpine Presbytery, New Zealand*

With great aplomb, Robert shares his keen insights into this wonderful Psalm, bringing streams of living water to the reader. I am truly proud to be able to publish *The Ripple Effect* in our Christ-Light Books imprint.

— *Jo Holloway, author of "Dance of Eagles"; screenwriter, script editor, publisher and book shepherd.*

ACKNOWLEDGEMENTS

Acknowledgements are, as always, due to Margaret, my ever-patient wife who has helped with many words and phrases; Charlie Jemmett, a literary expert who has worked on these words on the manuscript; my colleague, Reverend Laurence Ennor, who has assiduously checked my theology; and editor supreme, Jo Holloway of Sunpenny Publishing.

They have all listened well and given me excellent advice, most of which I have taken with thankfulness!

INTRODUCTION

As you read this book, you will find that the six verses of the twenty-third psalm have now become thirteen chapters, of varying lengths.

Plucking out the relevant segments, Robert has examined other Biblical scriptures to find out what this psalm is saying about our Almighty and Amazing God.

So read on, and you might enjoy the same rippling effect!

Psalm 23:1-6
Good News Bible

1. The Lord is my shepherd; I have everything I need.

2. He lets me rest in fields of green grass and leads me to quiet pools of fresh water.

3. He gives me new strength. He guides me in the right paths, as he has promised.

4. Even if I go through the deepest darkness, I will not be afraid, Lord, for you are with me. Your shepherd's rod and staff protect me.

5. You prepare a banquet for me, where all my enemies can see me; you welcome me as an honored guest and fill my cup to the brim.

6. I know that your goodness and love will be with me all my life; and your house will be my home as long as I live.

Psalm 23:1-6
King James Version

1. The Lord is my shepherd; I shall not want.

2. He maketh me to lie down in green pastures: he leadeth me beside the still waters.

3. He restoreth my soul: he leadeth me in the paths of righteousness for his name's sake.

4. Yea, though I walk through the valley of the shadow of death, I will fear no evil: for thou art with me; thy rod and thy staff they comfort me.

5. Thou preparest a table before me in the presence of mine enemies: thou anointest my head with oil; my cup runneth over.

6. Surely goodness and mercy shall follow me all the days of my life: and I will dwell in the house of the Lord for ever.

1

Psalm 23:1

The Lord is my shepherd;
I shall not want.

David, the vibrant psalmist? Or the caring shepherd?

Maybe both!

The young Israelite David walked many miles up hill and down dale, leading the sheep to fresh pastures and gurgling streams. He searched for those lambs straying from their mothers, or for sheep fallen down a gully and unable to get out. He lay down in front of the sheepfold, guarding the flock from marauding wolves, hungry lions, and not-so-friendly bears, to become aware that God was *his* heavenly Shepherd.

David commences his psalm with a big bang! The order of this opening stanza is very carefully constructed. It starts off with *The Lord is my Shepherd* and not *My Shepherd is the Lord.*

You may think I am making a finickity distinction, but it needs to be made, for it guards against a very real trap today – the term "O My God."

This is so ho-hum that most of the media screen characters are using it like a mantra. Indeed, they have formed a worldwide club where they use the now shortened three-letter term "OMG" as a sort of general exclamation expressing disbelief, frustration, excitement or even anger. They are telling us that, whatever their god may be, it is a human god made in their own image.

Christians experience God in and through our own lives, expressing "O My God" (but certainly not OMG) in praise and thanksgiving to God.

Yet the God whom we worship is far greater than any experiences that we may have!

That is what David was saying here. He carefully acknowledges that *his* God was the One who broke into his human experiences, working through with love.

In fact, David is laying the foundational statement of Israel from Deuteronomy 6:4, *Hear O Israel; the Lord is our God, the Lord alone.*

The Hebrew for Lord is Yahweh, or Jehovah. Nowhere is it used without the prefix *The,* or *O, the Lord*, or *O Lord*. When God speaks, it is to say "I, *The* Lord" or "I am *The* Lord."

I have said that otherwise we run the risk of thinking that *all* human experiences play a part in the formation of God to be everything that *we* want. Indeed, there is an interesting progression in how God is revealed.

Often, the word *God,* is used by itself. In the two creation stories in Genesis, the word for God is *Elohim.* Though used in the singular form it is actually plural in nature – a reminder that "it is by faith that we understand that the universe was created by God's word, so that what can be seen was made out of what cannot be seen" (Hebrews 11:3). Hence the original Genesis statement (1:26-27), "Let *us* make man in *our* image."

Frequently, the word *God* is used with the title "Lord" beside it. It was the *Lord God* who walked through the Garden of Eden with Adam and Eve each evening (Genesis 3:8).

However, we find that later, there is an interesting change in the use of God's name.

When God reveals Himself to Moses at the burning bush, He had been saying until then, "I appeared to Abraham and Isaac and Jacob as Almighty God, but I did not make myself known to them by my holy name" (Exodus 6:3).

And what was that holy name? It was Jehovah, the Lord, *I Am who I Am,* used in the sense that the almighty God, the *Elohim,* is personal.

One can sense David's excitement as he parades the nature of the One who shepherds him as *the Lord God Almighty!*

This is a God who wants to deal with people in a new way. The first thing we do is set a guard on our tongues that they might be faultless, our eyes that they might not catch sight of anything abnormal, our minds that they won't be open to influences which are outside of self-control, and our sexuality that it might be blameless.

A tough assignment!

Remember the prophet Isaiah? He stands before God and hears those wonderful words of the worshipping angels: *Holy, Holy, Holy is the Lord God Almighty.*

However, Isaiah's immediate response was, *I am a man of unclean lips and I live among a people of unclean lips, for my eyes have seen the King* (Isaiah 6:3-5).

If it is true that the Lord God is our Shepherd, does it then mean that God is only Shepherd? No, of course not! That is simply one aspect of God in the scriptures. There are many more facets of God's eternal-being.

This is what the Lord, the eternal I AM, says of Himself:

I am the Lord, Creator of all things – Isaiah 44:24.

I am the Lord, I speak the truth – Isaiah 45:22.

I am the Lord, there is no one else – Isaiah 45:18.

I am the Lord, and not man – Hosea 11:9.

I am the Lord, God of all flesh – Jeremiah 32:27.

I am the Lord, your holy God – Isaiah 43:15.

I am the Lord, who makes you holy – Leviticus 20:8.

I am the Lord, I do what is just and right – Jeremiah 9:26.

I am the Lord, at work in this land – Exodus 8:22.

I am the Lord, who has made you my own people – Exodus 31:13.

I am the Lord, your saviour – Isaiah 49:26.

I am the Lord, who forgives sins – Isaiah 43:25.

I am the Lord, who strengthens you – Isaiah 51:12.

I am the Lord, who answers prayers – Zechariah 10:6.

I am the Lord, who heals you – Exodus 15:26.

I am the Lord, who changes not – Malachi 3:6.

Out of the sixteen scripture quotations above, David had no idea of eleven of them, for they had not yet been written!

I suppose that when David was detailing *the Lord is my Shepherd*, it was not to limit God in any way to just being a shepherd. David invites us to broaden our vision of who God really is. When you think about it, all that has been revealed of God is all we could possibly need of God!

The Lord God was not just our Shepherd yesterday or last week, but our Shepherd today and every day into eternity.

It is because God is who He is, that God does what God does and will do, evermore!

Well, if David was getting moved about God from just this limited perspective, then there is ample opportunity for us to be thrilled about God from what the rest of the scriptures reveal.

Because God is always the great Creator, it means that there is no room for any other gods. God is always a holy God. God is always helping us to grow in our understanding of Him and His ways.

God is always our Saviour and, therefore, He forgives all sins. God always provides comfort and strength to us. God always answers our prayers whatever form the answer may take. God is always able to heal us and therefore, God never changes!

What a God!

Surely, like David, our hearts, our souls, our very being, hungers and thirsts for a God like that!

But hold on! David continues to speak of his personal attachment to the Lord, to the "I Am" Shepherd. "The Lord," he triumphantly says, "is *my* Shepherd."

As we have seen, David doesn't use "my" in any sense of ownership, but in a realisation that it is possible to be in a living relationship with this marvellous God as Eternal Shepherd.

It also means that, if David is to follow his Shepherd's directions, he must be listening for God's voice and therefore be obedient when he hears it. Being aware of the eternal *IS-ness* of God is a living relationship!

So, how do we have a living relationship with this great, eternal Lord? Through Jesus, the Messiah.

That which has been revealed of God *is* embodied in the person of Jesus Christ, who displays bodily the fullness of the Godhead.

Take a look at the letter to the Philippians, chapter 2. Paul personifies all that Jehovah the Lord is in heaven, and is the same now on earth. That is why Jesus made the startling statement about Himself: *Before Abraham was born, I AM* (John 8:58). He takes the holy name of God and applies it to Himself.

Jesus also declares that He is *the light of the world* (John 8:12), *the living bread* (John 6:35, 41, 48, 51), that He *came from above* (John 8:23), is *the door/ gate of the sheep* (John 10:7), *the good Shepherd* (John 10:11, 14), *the Son of God* (John 10:36), *the resurrection and the life* (John 11:25), *the way, the truth and the life* (John 14:6), and *the true vine* (John 15:1).

All this is encapsulated in the Gospel of John 3:16, when God says that His dear Son is to be sacrificed for us, and therefore the cross becomes the everlasting link.

In Jesus we not only find the true nature of God being revealed, but through Him, we can be recreated (born again) and thus, made holy.

We can set out on a path of justice and righteousness.

We can come to know God's saving power and receive forgiveness all the time.

We can be lovingly comforted and become stronger. We can also have our prayers answered and be healed both physically and spiritually, for our God changes not! And because it was a factual reality, David sang with all his might what he had discovered: *The Lord is MY Shepherd!*

2

Psalm 23:2

He maketh me to lie down in green pastures; he leadeth me beside the still waters.

In my youth, I attended the Keswick Christian Convention each summer. One of my favourite hymns came out of the Keswick Book: hymn 9, in the "Longing for Holiness" section.

In the first verse, it says: *My Saviour, Thou hast offered Rest, Oh give it then to me: the rest of ceasing from myself, to find my all in Thee.*

Looking in my dictionary, I found the verb *rest* means a whole host of things like ceasing work, to relax, to recover, to slumber, or even, sleep. In the noun section, it means a period of resting. That is a good explanation.

I went to other translations of this verse. David says, *lie down in green pastures,* or another, *God leads us beside still waters,* or even, *God allows us to rest in fields of green grass;* and finally, *renew ourselves by quiet pools of fresh water.*

The New English Bible gives a different take: *He makes us lie down in green pastures, leading us beside the waters of peace.*

Paul Achtemeier, an American theologian, puts it another way: *In grassy meadows, He makes me repose; by restful waters He leads me.*

David knows that *his* Shepherd always brings security and refreshment, and invites us to have an internal rest which is so real that it will sustain us during any stress, ailment or tragedy, and through every age and circumstance.

This reflects on God's mighty character, for He *never* ceases work, or relaxes, or slumbers, or even sleeps.

The Shepherd God is so vigilant that He attends to all the needs of the people of God to this day!

No shepherd worth his salt, let alone the Shepherd God, would want anything else except the best for his flock, and that will mean *all* that we need, wherever we are and in whatever situation we may find ourselves.

This is the desire of God for you and me: to provide rest forever!

Wow!

What about our Saviour Jesus Christ, who offers us such rest? *Come unto me,* He says, *All you who are weary and heavy-laden, and I will give you rest* (Matthew 11:28-30).

You see, I had goosebumps when I realised that *He Himself* – or as much as we can cope with at this moment – gives eternal rest.

I quickly turned my attention to another realisation – God's rest is *shared.* The Book of Genesis tells us that in six days God created the earth and the

19

heavens, and then He rested.

From what?

His rest was not just a reaction to His exacting work. No, it was intended to be a shared rest with two others, Adam and Eve.

Each evening they *rested* in God's presence as they *walked* together in the garden of Eden, forming a wonderful relationship.

We get a glimpse of that relationship in Exodus 33:14. Most translators use *rest* and relate it to God's Presence. However, in verse 18 of the same chapter, Moses sees the dazzling light of God's presence.

Does this mean that this is what rest is – communion with Him? After all, this is what we were designed for!

I rushed to see that God's rest arises out of God's promise.

In Exodus 3:1-5, Moses talks with God about the enslaved Israelites.

One day while Moses was taking care of the sheep and goats of his father-in-law Jethro, the priest of Midian, he led the flock across the desert and came to Sinai, the holy mountain. There the angel of the Lord appeared to him as a flame coming from the middle of a bush. Moses saw that the bush was on fire but that it was not burning up. "This is strange," he thought. "Why isn't the bush burning up? I will go closer and see."

When the Lord saw that Moses was coming closer, He called to him from the middle of the bush and said, "Moses! Moses!"

Moses answered, "Yes, here I am."

God said, "Do not come any closer. Take off your sandals, because you are standing on holy ground. I am the God of your ancestors, the God of Abraham, Isaac, and Jacob." So Moses covered his face, because he was afraid to look at God.

We can sense that behind the boldness of Moses' words, there was also an insecurity in his heart, so he asked God what His plan was for leading the people into the promised land.

God's reply in Exodus 3:12 was: *Surely I will be with you... I will go with you for I will give you rest – and as much as you need.*

How does this fit in with everlasting rest?

Although Moses had a whole succession of enemies to deal with, this was God's promise: His eternal presence.

On my trusty computer, I was listening on YouTube to one of Rachmaninoff's Piano Concertos. A classical music aficionado comments in the scroll beneath, "I started out thinking that this piece is too slow. About five minutes later this changed to – I've been listening too fast."

It is so easy for Christians to find reasons for "listening too fast" and not receiving the shared renewal of worship.

Admittedly, the realities of modern life confronting us may make it nigh impossible for us to take one single day as a day of rest and recreation. There is no excuse for us not to take quality time out, simply to rest with God.

Look at Psalm 131 where David, the shepherd and psalmist, warrior and king says in verse 2, *As a child lies quietly in his mother's arms, so my heart is quiet within me.*

This resting "in his mother's arms" is a loving rest, not just one day in the week or when we feel like it. It is an attitude of rest all the time. In fact verse 3 of the same psalm has it, *Trust in the Lord now and forever!*

In the Old Testament, God's rest comes through the Messiah, too! In Isaiah chapter 53, the Messiah Jesus was the pattern of God's rest. It is because Jesus is gentle and humble in spirit, that *As a lamb He was led to the slaughter and He opened not his mouth* (Isaiah 53:7 and following).

It was Jesus who was wounded for *our* transgressions, bruised for *our* iniquities, bearing *our* griefs and carrying *our* sorrows.

Through my various ailments I have been mulling over the example of Jesus' suffering. The apostle Peter wrote, *God will bless you... if you endure the pain of underserved suffering* (1 Peter 2:19b).

When I had the severe stroke, I accepted pretty quickly my ongoing difficulties from the magnificent, mysterious and almighty God.

In fact, I only had one thought – that God loves me through and through, and though I would not have any idea of the forthcoming consequences, I would rest in the knowledge of restful resting, before comprehending the eternal question of why!

This may not get answered – lost, I suppose, in the overwhelming magnificent, mysterious and almighty God! It is the relationship between us.

When my wife and I came into this part of the retirement home, we found that there were gorgeous flowers in the gardens surrounding the magnificent buildings.

There were caring medical and other staff from many nations wearing colourful, well-designed uniforms.

I have thick sweetened porridge for breakfast, then two choices of cooked meals at lunch time, plus morning and afternoon teas, and then supper.

Medication arrives, and staff check that we have swallowed our pills. Various types of buzzers, alarms and bells provide welcome communication. When the debilitating Covid-19 is around, they provide the latest technological wonders to keep us secure.

Laundry is collected and, when it is done, returned in perfect condition.

The village itself is quite large. It has an enormous atrium for relaxing in. There are two grand pianos, and various concerts are given by wonderful orchestras and outstanding soloists. You would think that we are in our heavenly home!

So, I have composed a verse on this very restful subject!

Lord! You sing to me
Your love songs – sharing songs
of life with me!
The music can be simple, or
profound as it can be.
Notes can speak in dying darkness,
or the deep rejoice in sound,
But the harmony's discovered
when the resting God is found!

3

Psalm 23:2

*He maketh me to lie down in green
pastures: he leadeth me beside the still
waters.*

It is always hard to communicate with
people, and to say what you want to
say so that what is said is *heard,* and
what is heard is *understood*, and what
is understood is what was intended in
the first place!

After peering over my shoulders to read
my notes, my wife and Chief Critic
raised a query – I had not actually
explained what *rest* was.

My response was that I have said that
God's rest is reflected by His own character, so His rest is holy and creative.

I further explained that God's rest arises from His own promise, something we can always be sure of.

Also, God's rest can be practically given to us by our taking quality time out of our stressful lives to share in on-going worship with perpetual renewal!

The way in which we can obtain that worshipful renewal is to look to our Saviour Jesus and find that He will share our griefs and bear the weight of our sorrows. In doing so, He carries all our burdens!

I added that we would miss out on God's rest if we did not respond to His invitation to receive that rest!

My Chief Critic shook her wise head, and looking steadily at me, responded.

"Yes. I know all about that," she said in her stentorian tones, "but you haven't said what rest *is!* Do you mean putting your feet up, or snuggling close beside me? Or is it a rest on the music manuscript when I play the piano?"

"No, of course not," I haughtily replied, my emphasis showing now in my person.

"God's rest is active and so it means entering and sharing His ongoing work of stability. God rests after creation, but He works diligently to keep the universe going. Being at rest in God's understanding means we get God's rest as well. See how restful I am!"

However, it had no effect on my Critic – Chief or not! She repeated her initial query: "You still haven't said what *rest* is," and going out of my study, she very firmly closed the door with a rattling sound.

Well, this was a challenge! What could I take from the following phrase in the psalm: *He restores my soul,* and relate it back to rest?

The word s*oul* divides humans into three distinctive parts – body, soul and spirit. The Hebrew word for soul is *nephesh.* The New Testament Greek word is *psyche.* Both encompass intellect and emotion. In other words, the soul represents the totality of human life.

Soul is used first in Genesis 2:7: *The Lord God formed man from the dust of the ground and breathed into his nostrils the breath of life and man became a living being* – ie a living nephesh (breath, soul).

In his Gospel, doctor and historian Luke relates Jesus' genealogy. He informs us that, as well as Jesus being the *Son* of God, Adam is also related to God as a *son* (Luke 3:38).

That doesn't mean that Adam had a physical, a mystical or even a holy relationship with God in the same way as Jesus had with His Heavenly Father or the Holy Spirit.

God *created* Adam. That meant that Adam was lower in a loving situation, but he *knew* and *experienced* the Living God with absolute freedom.

Unfortunately, that spiritual dimension became tainted by sin, leading on to corruption and death. It can only be restored through God's Spirit. For that restoration to take place, we are called to change direction, thus receiving from God a good and gracious gift.

In other words, being "born again."

The majority of people will not recognise God's free gift. Their constant response is, "We're OK. We don't need God in our lives."

That is not how God sees it. In the opening words of Mark's Gospel 1:15, Jesus says, *Repent, the kingdom of God is here.* The Gospel, the good news, bluntly speaks of *repentance*, to turn back, to change direction, or, to use David's words in this psalm, take the eternal *right* path.

However, I had the task of convincing my Chief Critic of the *rest* that she was carping on about. I went at it another way.

"When we had our lounge suite re-covered, our friends didn't say, 'Your lounge suite has been re-covered', but 'You have got a *new* lounge suite'. Such was the effectiveness of the upholsterer's work. I earnestly proclaimed, 'Will not God do the same for us?'"

Then, wanting to get the point home, I also said, "The Shepherd God's rest means to *refresh*. There are the advertisements for skin creams that show dry and brittle leaves, representing a realistic example of human skin. Then the advertisers show the amazing results of their skin cream.

"Our lives are often dry and brittle [just look at my reaction to my Chief Critic!], and there is always the need to be refreshed and moistened by God's constant anointing."

Then I said, "Resting has the idea of *rescue,* as well. Often," I reminded my wife, "we will not fully know the implications of our actions nor see the dangers ahead of us, but we are in constant need of being rescued from ourselves and our situations."

I recalled how, when I was working on a sheep farm in my younger days, a few sheep would always present me with a challenge.

"On opening the gate between the two paddocks, the flock would rush to eat more pleasant pasture. However, there was always one ornery sheep that managed to get firmly caught between the gate and the fence and hurt itself by ramming up against the gate post. I had to pick it up and carry it through the open gate. In other words, I rescued it. God always is on the watch to rescue us."

My wife looked as if my reasoning was beginning to sink in, so I quickly continued.

"Resting also means *retrieving* that which is lost. Jesus' parable of the lost sheep brings this concept to life."

My musical wife had just chosen a hymn for the Ladies Fellowship and had the music and words on the piano. I started to sing. "There were ninety and nine that safely lay in the shelter of the fold. But one was out on the hills away, far off from the gates of gold." (Lyrics by Elisabeth Clephane and music composed by Ira Sankey).

"Maybe," I said very carefully, "you have lost your hope, your joy, your peace and indeed, your ever-lasting patience! The Shepherd God will retrieve it for you!"

Tentatively, I raised the next point – *rest means to reclothe.*

"Have you ever dreamed of being naked in a public place?" I asked my wife. "No? It is, I am assured, a common dream. I imagine that it has its origins in Adam and Eve who found themselves naked, so they wrapped themselves with fig leaves, quick smart!"

My wife had a snigger at this and went away to do other wifely things.

The next day, I continued this friendly argument.

"When I had clinical depression, I was not coping with the constant noises in my head. The sensations and sounds of wriggling worms, plopping porridge, fizzing sherbet, periodic spot-welding, metal riveting and draught horses became louder and more persistent every pounding moment. I thought that the next downward step was madness. But I kept quiet, not wanting to reveal anything that would cause other people to think that I *was* mad.

"My thoughts ran rational and sane,

but soon they became dark and fore-boding – just like the man with demons whom Jesus healed." (Matthew 8:28-34, Mark 5:1-29 and Luke 8:26-39)

I said that without the clothing and always cutting himself, this poor demoniac was suddenly made free. His healing meant that he became re-clothed and in his right mind, so rest means to be *renewed*.

I continued. "After suffering the normal seasonal ailments like heavy colds, sore throats or atrocious 'flu, we men eventually arise from our sick beds and, having been renewed, we welcome life again, saying, 'I feel like a new person,' renewed into new strengths and fresh purposes."

I quickly pointed out that resting is a *reward*.

"There is a reward in the here and now," I told my wife. "It arises from our being in fellowship with the Shepherd's rich blessings. And there is a reward for faithful service which we render to God. His promises are a 'crown of righteousness' that He will give to us in glory, when we will hear the wonderful words, *Well done, good and faithful servant!"* (Matthew 25:23)

My wife thoughtfully said, "What you are talking about is being in a loving relationship with the God of our faith, and that *is* very emotional."

"Yes," I emphatically said. "If we really want to understand the concept, we can refer to Isaiah 57:15: *I am the high and holy God, who lives forever. I live in a high and holy place, but I also live with people who are humble and repentant, so that I can restore their confidence and hope.*

"How much understanding did the sheep have for the Shepherd? The sheep understood that the Shepherd was there to lead them to fresh water, providing green pastures for food, plus protection from harm. The sheep were in a right relationship with their Shepherd. He was theirs, and they were His."

Glancing at my wife I gave my final comment. "It is God's everlasting work to give Christian people eternal rest as they quietly go on munching from the green pastures."

My wife then gave me a very welcome kiss, and said, "Well done, you!"

I wondered what she would say when I tackled the next word in the psalm.

4

Psalm 23:3

He restoreth my soul: he leadeth me in the paths of righteousness for his name's sake.

Many people will have shared an experience of motoring with a back-seat driver. Maybe you have been one, offering your keen observations about the driving habits and dangerous speeds of other drivers. However, a back-seat driver who is also a map-reader can become catastrophic.

If dark nights and driving rain or persistent snow are added to the mix, then a journey along the *right* road to get to the *right* highway becomes a hazardous experience.

Yet David was saying, "God will lead us in the *right* path."

The Hebrew word for path is an interesting word. "A trodden way, a footpath, or an established way, or a course of life," so says Webster's Revised Unabridged Dictionary.

However, the Shepherd God does not lead us on just any sort of path – it is always on a path that is *right* in God's eyes.

King David was so enthralled by lovely Bathsheba, that he committed sexual sin with her while her husband Uriah, an elite soldier of David's troops, was still alive. David subsequently killed Uriah.

When David uses the word *right*, the word envelops both moral and physical decisions, as well as spiritual realities.

His Psalm 51 (a prayer for forgiveness for his actions) seems to make it so. It certainly took David a year or so to be honest with himself before he was able to return again to the right path.

But how do we know the right way to get onto the *right* path? We will not know the answer unless we are in a close relationship with the Shepherd God.

If our lives are not intimately intertwined with God, then we will never hear His still small voice saying to us: *This is the way, walk in it.* (I Kings 19:12 and Isaiah 30:21)

We need to be actively searching the Biblical principles of right-way-ness. I don't mean for the sake of just knowing what we believe in our church traditions but venturing forth into an ever-fresh future of intimate belief in God, who stands alongside us at all times.

I can remember that my Sunday school and Bible Class days were much more regimented than they would be today. I studied hard to learn the Shorter Catechism of 107 questions. Even though they were agreed upon by the "Assembly of Divines at Westminster and with Scripture Proofs," I only learned four, but I learned them thoroughly!

The Catechism starts off with this amazing question: "What is the chief end of man?"

The answer is, "Man's chief end is to glorify God and to enjoy Him forever."

The second query is, "What rule has God given to direct us how we may glorify and enjoy Him?"

The answer is, "The word of God... in the scriptures... is the only rule to direct us how we may glorify and enjoy Him."

By reading the Bible for ourselves, and discussing the everlasting truths with others, we can now appreciate and enjoy it forever.

It is like a flock of sheep, constantly grazing!

5

Psalm 23:3

He restoreth my soul: he leadeth me in the paths of righteousness for his name's sake.

There are many advertisements that blithely use the word *guaranteed*. This is where manufacturers and retailers put their reputations on the line by using the evidential word a lot.

However, the consumers of the products – us – are the ultimate judge of the worth of the guarantee. They will only be discovered in testing the product.

For me to speak of the Shepherd God in terms of modern retailing is dubious, but, in a very real way, this psalm does speak in a similar vein. It has the words, *For His own name's sake.*

What the psalm is telling us is that the honour, reputation, even the name of God, is tied up with what has already been told about Himself to the ongoing actions as the eternal Shepherd. "(God) restores my soul, leading me in the paths of righteousness... *for His own name's sake.*"

All that we need is what God will supply. All that we require, God will provide.

It implies that God is putting His own reputation on the line. God will satisfy us at the very core of our being "for His *own* name's sake."

See those amazing rippling words now, with new understanding!

Jesus calls Himself the Good Shepherd who would lay down His life for His sheep. He said, *This is my body, which is broken for you.*

We all know brokenness of one sort or another. We have all suffered broken hearts or shattered dreams. We have all shared to some measure in the fragmentation of our lives.

Yet, *this is my body*, says Jesus the Good Shepherd. *It has been broken for you, so that you can be restored and know the fullness of life. This is my blood, poured out for you, for the forgiveness of sins, so do this in remembrance of me.*

So, consider the facts about Jesus' life and ministry. About His death on the cross and His resurrection and ascension. He challenges us to make decisions about His claims. Rather than being professional sceptics, we now want to see *history* as being *His Story!*

Our Shepherd God does all this, for His own name's sake. He offers *Himself!*

Wow, again!

6

Psalm 23:4a

Yea, though I walk through the valley of the shadow of death...

There are many aspects of life which seem deathlike. I detailed some of them previously – broken hearts, shattered dreams, brittle relationships, dashed hopes, bitterness, age and illness. Now, we are here, within the valley of the shadow of death.

Years ago, in a wintry July, I was on a religious retreat in the countryside. Every day I would go along the narrow gravel road that meandered its way out of the Christian centre, by myself.

The road changes direction before it

dips down into a narrow valley, then crosses a ford through a gurgling stream. When the sun is up, it is a place of great beauty. Through the bare trees one can see a rich landscape of cream-coloured grass, freshly ploughed tar-black soil, greens of various vegetables, the browns of the hills, and the snow-capped mountains in the distance.

However, in the cold brisk morning, the swirling mist surrounds it so that this stark scene becomes a very dark, uninviting place. Trapped dank air, brittle ice that crackles underfoot, bracken and bare trees taking on strange and weird forms. This place of beauty now becomes a shadowland.

According to Moffatt's translation, it was the *Glen of Gloom*.

It is obvious that when this verse talks about the shepherd's rod and staff used actively for protection, that the psalm is primarily talking about being able to live fully now, in spite of other circumstances which may throw us off the mark.

A home with beautiful things can quickly become the scene of destruction, its privacy violated and tarnished beyond logical explanation. Roads can quickly become a place of accident, carnage, ambulance, police, undertaker, funeral and grief. People known for years can become unfamiliar and opponents to meaningful life. A partner to whom life was committed ended because of violated marriage vows. The peaceful sleeping of an infant is shattered when the cot becomes a deathbed.

They become now, our shadowlands.

The Bible doesn't give a full reason for there being shadows in life, but what it clearly teaches is that God shares the shadows with us, and that in those shadowlands, we find the Shepherd God is present.

Of course, the knowledge and understanding of that fact will not automatically remove the sense of violation that we may have experienced. The heartache will continue to eat at our soul for a long time, and the sorrows that unexpectedly overwhelm us, remain.

Some of us will say that the devil did it. In his book, *The Screwtape Letters,* CS Lewis (published by Geoffrey Bless, London, 1942), the knowledgeable Christian thinker, has Satan declaring that the greatest strategy he could undertake was letting people think he didn't exist. In that way, Satan could have complete freedom to exercise all his evil purposes.

The apostle Paul details in Romans 6:9,23, that the death of Jesus was to destroy the devil who has the power of human death. *The wages of sin is death, but the gift of God is eternal life in Christ Jesus our Lord.*

Logically then, if there was no real devil, there would have been no need for the death of Jesus, who, we are told, died to set us free from that evil (I Corinthians 6:11).

We often strive for the Holy Spirit's life-changing gifts and the everlasting fruit. To that end we have no problem with the belief that God's indwelling Holy Spirit works His transformation from the inside out. Many Christians seem to have difficulty in accepting the reality of people being under the influence of evil spirits.

Why do the scriptures then say to us that *the devil roams around, seeking whom he may devour* in 1 Peter 5:8, if such overtaking by the devil is not feasible?

Why do they tell now that we must *put on the whole armour of God* in Ephesians 6:13, unless there is something specific to resist?

Why are Christians warned to *protect themselves from the fiery darts of the devil* in Ephesians 6:16, if there are not any evil influences being shot in our direction?

We must remind ourselves that Jesus has *won* the battle against Satan, and so hold onto Jesus as we go through the skirmishes.

What skirmishes am I talking about? The Bible tells us that the failure to forgive can allow the spirit of criticism, or even bitterness, to take root.

Allowing the mind to be open to influences which include drunkenness, the taking of drugs or even hypnotism, can allow evil spirits to influence us.

Attending seances, or giving undue attention to horoscopes, can create a doorway for the spirits of divination.

Pornographic material can quickly become the murky environment for the spirit of lust to make its appearance.

The canny computer can have a disfiguring effect, as well. On YouTube, there is a great swathe of unhelpful information to viewers such as I. However, examine carefully what the meaning of this amazing truth is saying and, more importantly, how it is said.

However, perhaps one of the simplest forms of evil influence arises out of Christian illiteracy.

Remember, Jesus thwarted the devil by quoting scriptures. He knew the context of what He was saying. So, evil will succeed when we are ignorant of the truths of the Bible.

Our shadowlands are not necessarily the work of evil spirits, but I do say that we need to consider the danger that confronts us within these shadowlands.

I am not saying that the physical ailment, the brokenness of life, the stress that we are under, and the hopelessness that we often feel has evil origins, but I do say that circumstances can and will be used by evil forces.

Nor am I saying that, if we are subject to any evil influences, then God's Holy Spirit is powerless.

What we need to know is that Satan and his minions are defeated foes. The final battle is won by victorious Jesus on the Cross.

Now, you may not want to share with anyone what constitutes the deepest darkness, the shadowlands of your life.

You may not want to reveal those inner secrets to anyone.

However, I will tell you what the deepest darkness is.

Our shadowlands, our glens of gloom, are the inner aspect of our being that God is waiting to transform.

7

Psalm 23:4b

*I will fear no evil: for thou art with me;
thy rod and thy staff they comfort me.*

Before receiving my full set of expensive dentures, my dentist made sure that I was turned nearly upside down in his high-tech chair to explore my canal roots! On an X-ray, he noted two dark spots running from the top to the bottom of my tooth.

They were not carnivores struggling their way out of the depths of my cavities, but metal struts that had previously been put in to support the tooth.

This dental scene seems an appropriate approach to the end of the first part of the twenty-third psalm. *The Lord is my Shepherd* is the strut foundation one. Strut foundation two is: *I will not be afraid.*

This equation is central to David's declaration in the psalm. When the Shepherd is God, then He is our guide, provider, strengthener, protector, restorer and the light of our very being! There is no need to fear. Fear has no sway. Fear disappears for the Shepherd is here!

"Well, wait a minute," you might ask, raising your eyebrows. "Fear can be a positive thing. Fear helps life because, like pain, it is a necessity to guard against danger, and allows steps to be taken to avoid harm."

Yes, that is true, but unfortunately the type of fear I am talking about often turns and snaps at us. Instead of being part of our normal physical defence system, fear can become an unstoppable force that may take us over.

In the majority of verses, the Old Testament uses the word *fear* in a religious way. It describes one of the most basic responses of people who recognise their total unworthiness in the light of God's complete holiness.

When human sinfulness is put alongside God's absolute purity, then we must feel fearful. I have already quoted the cry from Isaiah, *Woe is me,* when God fills the temple in which Isaiah is worshipping. He says, *I am a man of unclean lips, and I dwell in the midst of a people of unclean lips* (Isaiah 6:5).

The New Testament does not silence the Old Testament revelation of the nature of God in any way. The scriptural concept of the fear of God must be altered to recognition of the loving acts of God.

Look at the cross. God loved the world so much that He turned His anger and justice on *Himself* when Jesus bore our sinfulness in His own body.

No. I repeat that the type of fear that I am talking about is completely different. This is a fear that eats away into the very core of our being, warping, disrupting, falsifying, irrational and sometimes completely meaningless. No wonder many human disorders use the New Testament Greek word "phobia" to describe fear.

But it doesn't end there, for fear also separates people from God and people from other people.

So, what can we do about this fear? These Bible passages might be of help to you.

Fear arises out of *vulnerability*, of having one's actions exposed for some misdemeanour. Look at Adam and Eve's sinful situation in Genesis 3:8-13. They didn't know what the ongoing situation would be.

Fear also rises out of *jealousy*. Perhaps the actions of other people are more appreciated than ours. The discomfort may grow into fear of others. King Saul discovered this ongoing weakness with the young and outgoing David. 1 Samuel 18:6-9, 12-15 and following passages.

Fear can be triggered by the *circumstances* of life. We may toddle along day after day without experiencing any major upsets, when suddenly disaster strikes without any apparent reason. That was Job's fearful experience when he was caught up in his suffering and hardship in Job 21:5,6.

Fear can arise from *other people's fear* so the phobia of others can be catching.

In Isaiah 8:11-14, the prophet spoke of fear in his own day. It was not different to the evil that seems to lurk around each corner waiting to pounce on us.

The universal news media always seems to find it quite easy to engender fear.

When I had clinical depression followed by a severe stroke, my understanding of life suddenly showed strange perspectives. Previously, I would look at the daily news and quickly sum up what was true, or not.

After these terrible ailments though, all I could find was a fearful agenda. It took some time before I started to recognise what *real* fear was. It was quite different to what the media presenters and local and overseas correspondents considered fear ought to be.

By going to other TV channels including Al Jazeera and the Christian ones, and by contrasting radio stations and serious publications including religious ones, I could see different perspectives coming from the same dire situations. It was only a simple task, but what I garnered of my fearful situation became much easier for me to cope with.

What people *think and say* becomes a fearful force for many of us. Instead of working through a family tragedy, or giving help where needed, the first reaction for some of us will be, "What will the neighbours think?" (See Ezekiel 12:6–11):

> *This is what the Sovereign Lord says: Strike your hands together and stamp your feet and cry out "Alas!" because of all the wicked and detestable practices of the people of Israel, for they will fall by the sword, famine and plague.*

Fear also comes from *dreams*. So often the things that we hide from our rational selves and are hidden from others, haunt our night-time dreams. Nightmares. Terror. Irrational fear.

In Daniel 4:4-5, he dealt with all that when he was called upon to help King Nebuchadnezzar, who was unable to sleep.

> *I, Nebuchadnezzar, was at home in my palace, contented and prosperous. I had a dream that made me afraid. As I was lying in bed, the images and visions that passed through my mind terrified me.*

Fear also comes out of *low self-esteem*. There is a tremendous lack of personal esteem in our society. People judge themselves alongside others, who, if the truth were known, are just as fearful as they are. Jesus addressed this type of fear in Matthew 10:26-31:

> *So have no fear of them, for nothing is covered that will not be revealed, or hidden that will not be known. What I tell you in the dark, say in the light, and what*

you hear whispered, proclaim on the housetops. And do not fear those who kill the body but cannot kill the soul. Rather fear him who can destroy both soul and body in hell. Are not two sparrows sold for a penny? And not one of them will fall to the ground apart from your Father. But even the hairs of your head are all numbered. Fear not, therefore; you are of more value than many sparrows.

Fear also surfaces when we take up *new ventures*. Perhaps starting on a new job or having to deal with difficult circumstances.

Often, we know what God is calling us to do but are afraid to answer His call because it may mean venturing into unknown territory.

Peter discovered the reality of that type of fear in response to Jesus' call when he tried to walk on water. As he responded to Jesus' word, "Come," Matthew 14:27-33, Peter soon found it was important to keep his eyes on Jesus, not the watery grave!

But immediately Jesus spoke to them, saying, "Take heart; it is I. Do not be afraid."

And Peter answered him, "Lord, if it is you, command me to come to you on the water." He said, "Come." So Peter got out of the boat and walked on the water and came to Jesus.

But when he saw the wind, he was afraid, and beginning to sink he cried out, "Lord, save me." Jesus immediately reached out his hand and took hold of him, saying to him, "O you of little faith, why did you doubt?" And when they got into the boat, the wind ceased. And those in the boat worshiped him, saying, "Truly you are the Son of God."

As well, fear arises from *old age*. Being older brings maturity and gracious wisdom, but the inability to do the things for oneself that were done in the past means a loss of independence.

I am getting used to the carers, nurses and the doctor constantly interrupting me from my daily tasks on the computer or waking me up from a pleasant slumber. King Solomon learned a lot about old age and wrote about it rather graphically in Ecclesiastes 12:1-5a:

So remember your Creator while you are still young, before those dismal days and years come when you will say, "I don't enjoy life." That is when the light of the sun, the moon, and the stars will grow dim for you, and the rain clouds will never pass away. Then your arms, that have protected you, will tremble, and your legs, now strong, will grow weak. Your teeth will be too few to chew your food, and your eyes too dim to see clearly. Your ears will be deaf to the noise of the street. You will barely be able to hear the mill as it grinds or music as it plays, but even the song of a bird will wake you from sleep. You will be afraid of high places, and walking will be dangerous. Your hair will turn white; you will hardly be able to drag yourself along, and all desire will be gone. We are going to our final resting place, and then there will be mourning in the streets.

Finally, people are afraid of *death.* Again, not so much the *fact* of death, but the *how* of death. *Will I die with dignity?*

Paul, in Romans chapter 8, wrote quite clearly that not even death can separate us from the love of God. Whatever the cause of our death, our loving God will accompany us. See also Hebrews 2:14-15:

Since the children, as he calls them, are people of flesh and blood, Jesus himself became like them and shared their human nature. He did this so that through his death he might destroy the Devil, who has the power over death, and in this way set free those who were slaves all their lives because of their fear of death.

Fear of exposure, from jealousy, from life's circumstances, by other people's phobias and what other people might say; fear from dreams, low self-esteem and how we have responded to God's call; fear of old age and, finally, death.

What a list of fears – and that is only some of them. How then does God disperse fear?

We should again peer into the word *fear* or *afraid*. Open Genesis 15:1, and we find that fear is dispersed by God's *protection*. Abraham heard the Lord say to him,

> *Don't be afraid, Abraham. I will shield you from danger and give you a great reward.*

God was Abraham's shield and defender by God's everlasting defence!

In Exodus 14:13, fear is dispersed by God's *salvation*.

As they stood between the Red Sea and the Egyptian army, between their future and their end, the Israelites were threatened with destruction. However, Moses cried out,

Don't be afraid! Stand your ground and you will see what the Lord will do to save you today. The Lord will fight for you. There is no need for you to do anything.

And in Leviticus 26:6 and John's Gospel 14:27, fear is dispersed by God's *peace*. The Lord said through Moses,

I will give you peace in your land and you will sleep without being afraid of anyone. And Jesus said, Peace is what I leave with you; it is my own peace that I give to you...

In Proverbs 2:6 and Deuteronomy 1:17, fear is dispersed by God's *wisdom*. From Him comes knowledge and understanding so that many Israelite leaders were able to make decisions allowing them to have wisdom "from on high."

It is the Lord who gives wisdom; from him come knowledge and understanding.

And:

> *Show no partiality in your decisions; judge everyone on the same basis, no matter who they are. Do not be afraid of anyone, for the decisions you make come from God. If any case is too difficult for you, bring it to me, and I will decide it.*

In Joshua 1:9, fear is dispersed by God's *presence*. Joshua was told: *Don't be afraid or discouraged, for I, the Lord your God, am with you wherever you go.*

As Joshua took over leading Israel into their new nation, his fear of the magnitude of the task was dispersed by God's ever-loving presence.

Or Isaiah 51:7-8, fear is dispersed by God's *teaching.*

> *Listen to me, you have... my teaching in your hearts. Don't be afraid when people taunt and insult you; they will vanish like moth-eaten clothing. The deliverance I (God) will bring will last forever.*

Or what about Psalm 27:1 and John's Gospel 1:5 where fear is dispersed by God's *light?*

Life's struggles, grievous afflictions and constant enemies have been the lot of people throughout the ages, yet, *the Lord is my light and my salvation, therefore I will fear no one!* or, *When the light of God's glory shines in the darkness, then darkness will never put it out,* is John's take on this.

In Romans 8:15, fear is dispersed by God's *Spirit... That Spirit that God has given you does not make you slaves and cause you to be afraid.*

And in I John 4:18, fear is dispersed by God's *love.... God is love, and there is no fear in love, for perfect love – as His love is perfect – drives out all fear.*

God's love places a guard around us in order to keep fear away.

Lastly, in 2 Timothy 1:7, fear is dispersed by God's *power.*

The type of fear Timothy had is rightly translated as "timid." Paul reminds

Timothy of how he had hands laid on him for his commissioning and how he had been endowed with God's Spirit, giving him power, love, and self-discipline.

Timothy's timid fear was dispersed by God's power. Because of that fact, there is no need to be ashamed or be frightened of testifying for the Lord.

So, how does God disperse the fears that assail us? By His protection, salvation, peace, wisdom, presence, teaching, light, Holy Spirit, love and power. Sounds good to me!

And what is in the middle of these two foundational struts?

It is the cross that is the link. Fear meets its match there.

8

Psalm 23:5

Thou preparest a table before me in the presence of mine enemies: thou anointest my head with oil; my cup runneth over.

Is God one of those hosts who is always over-effusive, poking His nose into the affairs of His guests? Or is He one of those humourless people who seem to resent any guest, pointing directions and saying as little as possible?

The psalm proclaims:

> *You prepare a banquet for me, where all my enemies can see me; you welcome me as an honoured guest and fill my cup to the brim* (verse 5).

Why did David change the metaphor so suddenly? I would say that to have a rich relationship with God is far more wonderful than using one metaphor alone, thus David wanted a wider picture!

When I was at United Theological College, part of my studies were the psalms of David.

In the composition of Psalm 22, apart from those words that Jesus used on the cross: *My God, my God, why have you forsaken me?* (Psalm 22:1), the psalmist goes on to say:

> *All nations will remember the Lord. From every part of the world, they will turn to Him; all races shall worship Him* (Psalm 22:27).

Then, Psalm 24 starts off by saying:

> *The world and all that is in it belongs to the Lord; the earth and all that live on it are his* (verse 1);

to the last verse:

> *Who is this triumphant Lord? – He is the great King* (verse 10).

With much excitement, I said to the college lecturer that it almost seems that a wise editor has now put the personal psalm, the 23rd, between these two great hymns of ascension.

Indeed, when Jesus attended the meal at the Pharisee's home, He comments on how the guests were jostling each other for the honour of a place near the head of the table, instead of simply accepting where they were put.

Jesus then told them a parable of a wedding feast in which He overturned the normal human criteria for establishing recognition and position in society.

Jesus was sharing a wide view of God's desire to serve the needs of the weak, the poor and the people without any hope.

Blessed are the poor, Jesus said, *for the kingdom of God is theirs,* as Matthew 5 and Luke 9 have it, and following.

Blessed are they that mourn, He said, for they will be comforted.

Blessed are the meek, He said, for they will inherit the earth.

Blessed are they who hunger and thirst after righteousness... for they with be filled with hope.

Yes, we, with our different vulnerabilities and with little power or clout or position or wealth or skills, or even health, are welcomed into our Host's presence, and there, Jesus bestows on us an honour which we can never deserve.

From my parish ministry, I can remember the great pleasure of noting the progress of a remarkable romance, and then officiating at the wedding of two youth leaders.

Once the couple had said "I do" to each other, I felt a great sense of *awe*. I had been given the actual spiritual and legal authority to declare them husband and wife, and therefore, as I made that declaration, I felt an almost overwhelming surge of *honour!*

Of course, I had been granted that position by someone higher – both bride and groom were relatives to a wide clerical heritage. Six parish ministers were present to make sure that I conducted the wedding service correctly!

As the church minister, I would never belittle the smiling congregation or, indeed, the bright couple standing before me, but I had a good idea that all the people there were well perfumed with hardy tincture!

From ancient times to modern occasions the world has known the custom of using sweet smelling oils and ointments, mainly to satisfy the needs for hygiene and personal attractiveness. The Israelite kings and priests were anointed with holy oil when being set aside for religious duties.

I was just browsing through my Bible dictionary, as you do, and I found that "making fat" is only used once in the Old Testament. It refers to an anointing which is not an external work of God but an internal work.

When we relate this psalm to the phrase about *the cup running over,* we start to get the picture – God feeds us from the "fat" of His table.

Neat, isn't it!

Returning for a moment to the married couple's wedding reception, I sampled the diversity of the main courses, the richness of the delicious pavlova, its decorative plate encircled by fruit salad and topped off with whipped cream.

As my mother constantly reminded me, *foo the noo* (for the now) from God's nourishing platters!

9

Psalm 23:6a

*Surely goodness and mercy shall follow
me all the days of my life...*

The television and newspaper media
are constantly reminding us in their
advertisements, "There's more!" and,
"There's much more!"

In the same way, what God says is that
He has *more* in His welcoming, *more*
in His bestowing with honour, *more* in
His giving us absolute protection and
more for our need of more satisfaction!

Don't we get excited by almighty God
who arranges things just for us, espe-
cially when it gives Him only pleasure?
(See Psalm 149:4)

I was reminded that Isaiah further says in chapter 55:2, *The Messiah will invite all the wretched and the poor to come and eat without having to pay anything.*

All of them share in God's hospitality.

Then the apostle John writes in a similar vein in Revelation. He sees a wonderful picture of the end when *all* of God's people worship Him, saying, *Blessed are those who have been invited to share in the wedding feast of Jesus, the Lamb* (19:6-9).

What a wonderful picture!

We have not finished yet. No meal is prepared without cost. There is the cost of producing the raw materials that go into the finished product. There is the cost of purchasing those same ingredients for those exquisite recipes. There is the messy cost of cooking the food.

There is also the cost of physical work in arranging tables and chairs, plus decorations, as well as the cost of clearing up afterwards.

In Isaiah's picture, God says He bore *all* costs, forever! In John's picture, the feast cost nothing either.

Some of us still remember that the bride's father customarily bore all the cost. The same in heaven for the redeemed – us, His bride – the cost of the Wedding will be carried by *God!*

Imagine, if you will, that we have a communion service.

We enter to Jesus' Table and share in the High and Holy moment.

We take the Bread of Jesus, His Body, which has been broken for us.

We share in the Cup of Christ, His Blood, shed for us.

We listen carefully to hear His words echoing down through history, *Do this in remembrance of Me.*

Apart from our individual appropriation of the bread and wine, it is a more meaningful and wonderful aspect of God's desire to meet the needs of *all* peoples with Himself.

It is one thing to take into our hands the elements of God's hospitality and be fed ourselves.

It is another thing to catch His heartbeat and feel the compassion that He has for the people of His world.

It is one thing for us to be internally satisfied, but it is another matter when we are so stuffed that we fail in our task to be the channel of God's hospitality to others.

In other words, the communion meal is a symbol of God's sacrificial generosity!

For a long time, Christians have had different perspectives about mission work.

Some have seen their task in purely spiritual ways with an emphasis on the "soul being saved" sort of thing.

Others have seen their primary task in meeting people's physical and educational needs.

However, I think that we need to remind ourselves that both aspects – spiritual and physical – are equal parts of the same Gospel.

We have already seen that no Jew would understand the division of body and spirit. We are a part of a unified personality, so what affects the body also affects the soul, and vice versa.

Any mother with a hungry crying child, or any wife with a household of hungry males, knows how cranky they can be until their hunger is met!

So, poverty, homelessness and hunger are not just physical matters but conditions which affect the total wellbeing of those who suffer. To be poor in food or clothing, in housing or employment, is also to be poor in spirit.

Mother Teresa of Calcutta said, "We give dying people bread, because they hunger and perish not just for bread, but also for love..."

So, when God shares from His Table, it is to feed the totality of the human person.

10

Psalm 23:6b

*... and I will dwell in the house of the
Lord for ever.*

Though dead now, Basil, our Labrador dog, had clear ideas about who was the most important person in our household.

Basil always looked with eager eyes and wagging tail as he waited to go for his morning walk. He accepted food from anyone who offered it to him. He would play with whoever wanted to be boisterous. However, the love of Basil's life was my wife. While each one of us would have our own respective place in his life, she was the *only one* that Basil adored.

From the moment my wife went out till the moment she returned, Basil stood guard at the window, his front feet on the sill and his mouth dribbling with eager anticipation. No matter how long she was away, five minutes or longer, my wife was always greeted as if her return was the most important thing to have ever happened!

To him, it was! She could make no movement in the home without the dog's eager eyes following her. Given the chance, Basil would live up to the saying "dogging her every footstep." We half-heartedly expect that he is waiting for us in heaven, his tail wagging as he waits for our joyful appearance!

There are two ways of looking at the word *follow* in this psalm.

Some dictionaries have it as *to run after; to chase and hunt.* Most translations of this verse use the word *follow* in the sense of God pursuing us.

Literally, that is correct. Many will know Francis Thompson's poem, *The Hound of Heaven,* where God is pictured as One who, with strong feet that followed,

followed after... who with unhurrying chase, and unperturbed pace and down the labyrinthine ways... until at the end, we get the words, *Rise, clasp my hand and come.*

Some of us can testify to God *hounding* us until we have been chased back to find again that place of safety and refuge. The concern that I have with the picture of *goodness and mercy* running after and chasing us in this way, is that it expresses "pursuit with hostile intent" – and that is most certainly not God's desire in this case!

There is a Bible passage where the apostle Paul's associate Demas said "no" and went away to other more interesting pursuits. It was only when Paul was imprisoned that we see Demas returning to the fold (Philemon 1:24). Was God following Demas with intent? But I digress.

Part of the solution to the word *follow* is in seeing it in a wider context.

Among all the various translations and paraphrases I have on my bookshelves are the *Good News Bible* and *Moffatt*.

The GNB says: *Goodness and love will be with me all my life.*

Moffatt gives an even wider picture: *Goodness and kindness wait* on *me* – not wait *for* me. He then indicates that the *following* is not a pursuit, but of goodness and mercy being our constant companions.

Imagine that we are at a high-class restaurant. Yes, I know that I have an inclination for excellent food in my thoughts, but remember, I constantly eat, so I will not take these examples away!

We can reasonably expect that the waiters of these restaurants will not only fulfil our requirements but will do so circumspectly and without fuss.

They will also give us good advice when we need it, and make sure that there is not an interminable time between courses.

There is no use going to a restaurant that has an excellent menu and an over-the-top cook preparing the meal if there is no one to take the meal from the kitchen to the table. It may get cold in the waiting so we might just as well have stayed at home and prepared our own meal, or got on the phone for a takeaway.

Goodness and mercy are God's Waiters. They serve with platefuls piled high with *honour* as an appetiser, *protection* as the entrée, *satisfaction* as the main course, and of course, *compassion* for dessert.

In the Old Testament, *goodness* has a wealth of meanings: beautiful, best, better, bountiful, cheerful, at ease, fair, glad, gracious, joyful, kindly, loving, merry, pleasant, precious, prosperous, wealthy and welfare.

Our waiter is the one who serves in beautifully clean attire, who attends to our needs better than another, whose actions are fair to both the owner and the customer, serving with a fine presentation and always glad to please the drooling patron!

This waiter is the one who is also gracious in approach, joyful in work, kind to difficult children, loves being with people and, therefore, is always merry, pleasant and precious.

In turn, the restaurant employer is prosperous simply because the waiter has earned it. Both have supplied the customers' requirements. Do you recognise any waiter of that calibre in that list?

Moving on, the Hebrew word for *goodness* is from the root *to do* or *to make*.

In other words, God doesn't simply arrange to give us all these aspects of goodness – it is part of His nature.

Take Moses' experience of God in the cleft of the rock. He asks God if he may see the dazzling light of His splendour. God literally replies (Exodus 33:18-23):

> *I will make all My goodness pass before you*

All of God's goodness is on display when we go into this heavenly restaurant.

God is the Host at the table of beauty. The best and better than anyone else!

God is bountiful and cheerful, making us at ease. God is fair and grants us His favours. God is loving, merry, pleasant, ever joyful and kindly towards us. And from His everlasting wealth, He seeks only our welfare.

Just soak in that imagery for a moment. Relax in God's presence as He waits on you with His goodness. Accept it all, for it is to *us* that God has given His great gift.

Most high-class restaurants have more than one waiter. So, too, with God who provides *Mercy* alongside *Goodness*.

In the Old Testament, mercy has a different meaning to the one in the New Testament, which has a legal application.

In Psalm 23, the word doesn't primarily have to do with God dealing with sin. Instead, mercy presents a different picture – *courtesy*. The basic meaning is to *bow the neck* as to an equal.

Our waiter, *mercy*, comes to us and, though in a serving capacity, he will not kowtow to us as an obsequious person would act, saying, "Yes sir, no sir, three bags full, sir or madam."

Our waiter confidently comes to hear our requests. "Yes, sir. Yes, madam. How can *I* help *you!*"

Because our waiter fully represents God our Host, then, as we bow the neck, we become elevated to a position higher than we really deserve. (Look again at Isaiah 57:15).

Then the word *mercy* has to do with *covenant*. There is an agreement between God and His people that the covenant is guaranteed to be effective forever. So, our waiter will provide the menu and allow us to make our choice within the realms of heavenly cuisine.

The menu will not allow us to take flights of fancy or order strange concoctions which are outside the skills of the cook. Nor will it upset the stomach and be harmful to our wellbeing.

The menu, the covenant, is more than enough, giving sufficient provision for all our needs.

The word *mercy* also has to do with the *compassion* God has for our weaknesses and our helplessness.

In terms of the meal, the waiter kindly overcomes our insecurities, explaining the menu's mainly French terms and gently compensate for our ignorance as to what wines can go with the food we have chosen.

The religious scholar William Tyndale (1495- 1536) wanted English people to have the Bible in their own language rather than the Latin tongue. He was executed for his faith but, before that, he translated mercy as "loving kindness."

Tyndale was possibly reflecting on Paul's letter to Titus: *When the kindness and the love of God our Saviour was revealed, He saved us, not because of any good deeds we ourselves have done, but because of* His own mercy (Titus 3:4).

Then the word mercy has to do with *consideration* – with a kindly disposition.

Our waiter recognises that the only reason the eager customers will be coming into this place is because the restaurant is open. They are serving us on the Host's behalf, so the waiter will act out of consideration for us.

Finally, God's goodness and mercy are still *waiting* on us to respond. He will not swoop on us the moment we are seated and before studying the menu.

Neither is God going away. Following us is God's main concern. His nature is to always *wait on tiptoes* until we are ready to respond.

11

Psalm 23:6

*Surely goodness and mercy shall follow
me all the days of my life: and I will
dwell in the house of the Lord for ever.*

During my pastoral ministry, I had
heard about and even shared in some
traumatic episodes. Often the trauma
is transformed by God's grace, like the
Christian woman who had just nursed
her faithful mother through the last
three months of her life.

Both mother and daughter believed
implicitly that, because of God's
unending love shown to them in Jesus,
there was a sure hope that the valley of
the shadow of death would be transformed by His ongoing presence.

The mother was rich in years and content with her life. But because she was virtually skin and bone and had the appetite of a sparrow, she wanted to escape her physical frailty and be with her Lord.

Although in command of all her faculties, she nevertheless tended to wander away from the reality of the moment. One day, she told her daughter that she had had a wonderful meal which had left her satisfied.

The daughter's initial response was, "Oh. Because you haven't eaten much, you just imagined it."

Then, as she thought further, she realised that her mother had been involved in an act which was part of the preparation for her death. She said, "Didn't Psalm 23 read, *You prepare a table for me, in the presence of my enemies?*"

When the daughter's Christian doctor was told of the experience, he responded, "You know what this means don't you?" and then repeated the same verse.

As fanciful as it may seem, this mother had shared in a heavenly meal that had been prepared for her, just before she entered into the perfect life.

Throughout the psalm, we find that the Shepherd God who leads His sheep, provides them with eternal water and excellent pasture, true guidance, right direction and safe protection. God is also the Host who provides us with safety and security.

However, at the culmination of this psalm, David transcends these physical limits, bursting into a song of heavenly life: "I will *live* in the house of the Lord forever."

This living will not follow the ways where guidance goes astray, protection is removed, quiet streams get polluted, scrumptious food goes off or waiters become impatient.

Our experiences of faith, joy, hope, wonder and praise in the here and now, will become now part and parcel of the glorious eternal there and then!

The Bible has an interesting progression in its unfolding of the nature of human death and eternal life.

The ancient Hebrews did not regard death as utter non-existence. No, death meant joining the departed in the underworld – *sheol*, a dreary, meaningless existence; a nothing world where one was cut off from the land of the living and from the presence of God.

That is why we read such *hopeless* expressions in King Solomon's Ecclesiastes when he continually says, "Life is useless!" or some such words.

However, take a look at the amount of God given wisdom that Solomon appreciated, and you will find that he doesn't say anything about the *rest* which God wants for him or human beings. Look at Genesis 2:2-4, Exodus 20:8-10, 23:12 and 33:14-18, and in the paraphrased version of the Living Bible the book of Hebrews chapter 4, and you will see what I am getting at.

However, when we read David's psalms, it is clear that the distress of death was not so much the fear of extinction, but that a loving relationship with God would suddenly be at an end. That, indeed, would be hell!

When the physical and the religious aspects of death come together, so to speak, it is seen as continued fellowship with God. Therefore, it is natural for there to be a connection between death and sin.

Ezekiel had these words to say – *The soul that sins... shall die* (18:4).

Yet the Old Testament clearly states that God takes no pleasure in human death, even of the extremely wicked. (Ezekiel 18:32 and 33:11).

On the other hand, Job, who suffered intense physical pain and emotional upset, was able to report, "I know my Redeemer lives – and I shall see Him!" (Job 19:25-27).

Because of the particular death of Jesus Christ, the insights of the Old Testament are amazingly deepened in the New, for the incredible happened. Through His resurrection, the immortal God destroyed death, for ever. As Paul described it: *Sin pays its wage: death; but God's free gift is eternal life* (Romans 6, 23).

Whatever is the actual cause of death, it is *we* who are still alive. David says, "*I* will live in the house of the Lord for ever" – and that is enough for me!

12

Rejoice!

The Triple Concerto

Composed for royal personages, Ludwig van Beethoven's Triple Concerto is written for three instruments – violin, cello and piano.

They alternately pluck out the allegro, largo and rondo notes and then, together entwine in a powerful crescendo of melodious music. A masterpiece!

In the same way, we have been playing the music of the twenty-third psalm, plucking out the various notes that form the grand finale of our scriptural Triple Concerto.

The first is *Sovereignty*. The psalm is primarily about God, who God is, what God's nature is, and how God acts as He relates to us.

It plucks out notes which say God is the Lord, the great I AM; the One whose very name is the guarantee that all that God says and does is eminently trustworthy and completely reliable.

Sovereignty has played, and is playing, a haunting melody which says to us that God is One who never gives up, who guides and provides for us, loves and cares for us so much, *that His mercies aye endure, ever faithful, ever sure.*

There is a book called *The Nature of God in Plain Language* (David L Hocking, USA, 1984). I know what the author is trying to do – to simplify the terminology and the way we think about God.

However, that is an impossibility, for the God of this psalm is totally beyond any simplification! We talk about Jesus the Messiah, who, as a human being, reflected the nature of God, but no matter how hard we explain it, we end up with a mystery.

What do the scriptures mean when they say, *In Christ the whole fullness of the God-head dwells bodily* (Colossians 2:9)? Or *God was in Christ, reconciling the world to Himself* (2 Corinthians 5:19) in the King James version?

This psalm very clearly and cleverly does not try to explain God, but accepts that God is at work, doing perfectly whatever God does.

This sovereign God, this supreme being, the heavenly God, tends to the needs of all His subjects, on a one-to-one basis. He doesn't stand aloof from us but is always drawing near to us.

As John explains in Revelation, *God's home is with human beings, He will live with them, and they shall be His people.*

I will be their God, and they will become My children, God triumphantly says (Revelation 21:3).

The second instrument is *Salvation.* Picking up the notes of sovereignty, it now weaves salvation with God's greatness and loving kindness.

So often we think of salvation as a single act. In terms of what Jesus did for us, salvation *is* one act – He died *once* and for all time on the cross for our sins.

However, in terms of ourselves, we see salvation in different ways.

When people commit their lives to Jesus, we say they have been saved. We rejoice when that happens. However, salvation is more than that. It is an ongoing process.

If my life was dependent on my original decision for Christ on the 10th of November 1957, or my missionary commitment to His service in 1961, then I would be saying that I haven't grown at all.

I did my missionary training with an Irishman from Belfast. He was a rather passionate sort of character. Indeed, one of his lady friends declared her lips were permanently damaged after he had kissed her!

This Irishman had an atrocious accent and he always abbreviated the term "brother" to "bro". Unfortunately, it always sounded like "bra" so when he asked someone "Are you saved bro," we always got a different picture than the term intended. A simple question became a dangerous instrument when he uttered it!

Now, if I was asked, "Are you saved bro?", I would want to reply that I have made many decisions for Christ and countless acts of commitment since those original dates I just gave you. That is the way it should be.

Because salvation is an on-going process, being saved starts off an eternal journey with the Saviour.

The same in this psalm concerto. We have two threads of interwoven music. We hear the strong notes of *sovereignty*, then, weaving its way, the melody brings evocative notes of *salvation*.

The question is, are we still experiencing an ongoing salvation, accepting free from Christ all that He has to offer from His everlasting storehouse of sovereignty?

Do we truly know that Jesus, the Good Shepherd, says, *I have come in order that you may have life – life in all its fullness?* (John 10:10).

To complete the psalm's theme, we now take up the notes of *Sufficiency.*

I have already hinted that there are TV advertisements where a certain breakfast food provider arranges with its producers to grow and send more.

Now, we are assured that there is an abundant supply and an ongoing sufficiency that God will provide all that we need, plus much more!

What the psalm's climax tells us is that salvation by the sovereign God is totally sufficient, not only because of the way that it comes to us, but because of the nature of the One providing that salvation.

It is because God is, that God will always have enough for now, and more when we need it, plus extra from His wonderful treasures.

Enough of what?

Of rest in fields in green grass. Of refreshment beside quiet pools. Of strength in times of weakness. Of guidance not just along any old path but on the right paths. Of God's promises which are guaranteed by God's Name.

Then a fear-free journey through our deepest darkness where we are continually protected, welcomed as an honoured guest and where we have the overflowing anointing of goodness and mercy in God's own house!

Sufficient Salvation from the Sovereign God in this spiritual triple concerto!

There is one last thing to draw from this psalm. David presents a *personal* testimony.

He starts off with the declaration that God is his Shepherd who supplies all his needs continually.

Then God leads and guides him by giving overflowing protection so that he won't be afraid, ever.

Then God always prepares the welcome cup which, surprisingly, is always full.

I wonder if on his dying day and shivering bed, David would have emphatically whispered, "The Lord is *my* Shepherd."

Knowing that His goodness and love are with him, and along with the affirmation that God's house will be his eternal home, David has everything that is needed, for eternity!

13

For Evermore!
Words by Robert Simpson
Tune: Greensleeves

Our loving God, our Shepherd now;
Our gracious Host to whom we bow:
Protection comes from Your great
power – Our enemies are defeated!

Refrain:
We shall live in His house, The House
Of God for evermore.
We shall always live with God –
God who loves and perfects us!

Goodness and mercy are a sign of life,
That breaks the realm of time.
Our Saviour won our victory –
The enemy death is defeated!

(Refrain)

Yes, all our sorrow, the grief and pain,
Beyond the grave they can't remain!
Life is but glorious with our God,
For immortality cloaks us...

(Refrain)

The Author

In *The Ripple Effect* Robert Simpson, a retired parish minister from Christchurch, New Zealand, reflects on the beauty of the Twenty-third Psalm.

This psalm has lived through many verbal and musical incantations down through the ages. The simple power of the psalm's imagery never fails to reaffirm the presence of the guiding hand of God.

Yet, considering all the Godly unknowns, and in spite of Robert's battle with clinical depression and electro-convulsive therapy, followed by a severe stroke, loss of speech, and limited mobility, he has, over time, found that the psalm's rippling effect has enabled him to praise and thank the eternal God!

Brought up in a Christian home, he initially worked at the Presbyterian Bookroom in Dunedin. Graduating from Auckland's Bible Training Institute, now Laidlaw College, he went to Port Moresby in Papua New Guinea as a literature missionary. There he met and married Margaret Sharman, an English medical missionary nurse and midwife.

They journeyed to England, where he was employed by a legal company, Butterworths of London, and later by the Prudential Insurance Company. With their four sons they then made their way to Sydney, Australia, where Robert graduated from the United Theological College, and where he commenced new parish ministries.

REFERENCES

Unless otherwise indicated, Scriptures and additional materials quoted are from the Good News Bible ©1994 published by the British and Foreign

Bible Society; and the Good News Bible ©American Bible Society 1966, 1971, 1976, and 1992.

The King James Version has also been used to illustrate the Psalm, and in places the author has paraphrased from other Bibles, including Moffat. All are used in alignment with copyright requirements, and/or fair usage.

When first published, the Good News Bible was designed in such a way that it had a limited vocabulary – "thought for thought" rather than "word for word" (Wikipedia GNB Beginnings). In

Papua New Guinea, where I worked as a literature missionary, people accepted this translation as "really good news". I still use the Good News Bible as the main means of communication between God and myself in New Zealand, and my writing reflects that in *The Ripple Effect.*

WEB PAGE FOR ROBERT SIMPSON:

https://www.christlightbooks.com/authors/
robertsimpson

MORE BOOKS BY ROBERT SIMPSON:

CROSSWAYS: *A memoir.* Following a stroke and clinical depression, Robert had a long road to recovery ahead of him, and he had to give up his parish and ministry to do so. This is the extraordinary tale of his battles and successes. He does not spare himself, but writes every raw detail as he relives it.

KALIMNA HEIGHTS: *A novel.* Based sometimes on actual stories and histories over the centuries, and sometimes a goodly sprinkling of imagination, the author takes us into one of the areas in which he worked as a minister.

PRIORITIES OF LOVE: *A novel.* This is a saga written around the adventures and otherwise of a family in New Zealand and England. An intriguing insight into the mind of a writer who never shies away from the extremes!